Playtime

Dorothy F. Shaw

Praise for Dorothy F. Shaw

"*Unworthy Heart* reminded me of what I love about the romance genre."—The Book Tart

"*Unworthy Heart* by Dorothy F. Shaw made me think, made my heart happy, made me tear up and made me sigh in happiness. Shaw combines heat with heart almost flawlessly. I cannot wait for the follow-up books in this series."—Romance Novel News

"I fell in love with the series from book one…Grab your copy and buckle up for the ride. Dorothy Shaw doesn't do anything halfway."—Beyond the Valley of the Books on *Defensive Heart*

"Holy smokes, can Dorothy Shaw write a freaking awesome sex scene…"—Wicked Good Reads on *Defensive Heart*

"*Defensive Heart* by Dorothy F. Shaw is a good read which gives credence to the statement that opposites do attract."—Harlequin Junkie

"Even though there is plenty of sex in *Shattered Heart*, the author does not neglect the storyline at all – packing it full of romance, danger, trauma, healing, laughs, and the Donnelly family."—Crystal's Many Reviewers

"*Shattered Heart* is an emotional tear-jerker of a romance that had me reaching for the tissues on more than one occasion." —Romance Novel News

"Wow! What a sexy, steamy story that kept me reading from the first page."—Crystal's Many Reviewers on *Stripped Bounty*

"If you are into vanilla, forget this book! Characters larger than life and sex to die for. Dorothy F. Shaw painted a canvas that is both intriguing and close to hardcore."—Amazon Reviewer on *Stripped Bounty*

"Epic story! Rosie and Badger are amazing characters that pull you into the story. The sex is HOT and the ending is perfect!"—Book Addicts PR on *Stripped Bounty*

"I was blown away by how easily the story was told by Dorothy F. Shaw"—CeeriJays Smexy HotReads on *A Few More Rules*

"*A Few More Rules* (a femdom novella) is a super-hot romance that sets the foundation well for a probable HEA between Rig and Beth. This story is a winner."—Romance Novel News

"WOW!!! This erotic, sensual short story will have you panting for more! These two beauties are more than fang bangers. The dark world of lust and sex will feed any appetite you desire."—Bookaholic and More Blog on *Playtime*

"I like books that grab my attention so much that I read a line and end up gasping or commenting out loud... and this one did just that - a few times! I'll definitely be reading it again."—Goodreads Reviewer on *Playtime*

"True to Dorothy Shaw's form, *Avoiding the Badge* is full of everything I love about her writing."—Amanda at Wicked Good Reads

"I liked the way the author brought about the truths that they had been keeping from each other, and I really enjoyed the steps that the two characters took in order to overcome the troubles in their path."—Amazon reviewer on *Avoiding the Badge*

"*Redeeming the Badge* is a second chance romance that is hot as Hades and with a backstory that will twist your heartstrings." —Amazon Reviewer

"This is a tale of love and heartache, dealing with some tough issues such as infertility, endometriosis, and miscarriage. It will tear at your heartstrings and make you believe in true love." —Amazon Reviewer on *Redeeming the Badge*

"Jeff and Tish are a good couple with incredible chemistry that makes you jealous. I can't recommend this series enough." —Amazon Reviewer on *Trusting the Badge*

"*Trusting the Badge* is a quick read for readers who enjoy a focus on relationship building, characters with tragic backstories, and some steamy moments." —Amazon Reviewer

"It was written in a way that I got very emotional reading it, most books don't make me cry. This one did."—Amazon reviewer on *Jaded Heart*

Playtime

© 2017 Dorothy F. Shaw

You're welcome…

High-powered executive, Dana Richards can't seem to get enough of his favorite exotic dancers at the Red Panther Gentleman's Club. RayAnne and Kyra are the feature act; putting on a vampire performance you can sink your teeth into--complete with fangs, and the sexual lure only a creature of the night can offer.

But when Kyra makes Dana a proposition he can't refuse, some intimate playtime, the arrogant executive gets more than he bargained for: The sex of his life. Plus two, undeniably real vampires.

Acknowledgments

To Shawna for her never-ending patience while editing me. To my marvelous ex-husband, TD Hoffman for plotting with me and for making me cover art. As always, you are awesome and I truly appreciate you. To Kyra, thank you for allowing me the use of your image and your name for my character. Much love to you.
To D.E., there are no words. Except maybe...
You're welcome.
Oh! And also, thank you. For everything. You rock.

Chapter One

RayAnne

"Ugh, he's so strange. He always says, 'You're welcome,' for no reason. It's like he thinks his just being there is something I should be thankful for."

"Who?" RayAnne buckled her platform shoe, stood and straightened her black, hooded cloak.

"That executive who always comes in here." Kyra zipped her micro skirt and then slipped on her heels. "It's just so… odd."

"Ignore him. He's an arrogant ass." RayAnne looked up. "Hurry! Mario just called for us on the overhead."

"I'm coming. I'm coming—shit!" Kyra skidded to a halt, her long, blonde-pink-and-black hair falling over her shoulder. "I forgot glitter! Oh! And mints!" With a quick spin on one foot, she ran back to her bag.

RayAnne rolled her eyes, crossing her arms over her chest as a beat of impatience spread through her. Oblivious to her annoyance, Kyra continued to dig in her bag in search of what she insisted were needed essentials.

RayAnne guessed they were, though. They might be real

vampires, blessed with eternal life and beauty, but they didn't sparkle on their own—despite what books or movies might indicate. The only thing they did under the great burning ball in the sky was burn...and not in a good way.

"Got it!" Kyra raised her arm in the air, proclaiming her accomplishment. "Blue or green?" She held up the two small bottles.

"Doesn't matter. Come on! The song is ending." RayAnne peeked through the curtains to the main floor. "Both work."

Kyra shrugged and then doused her neck, more than ample cleavage, and stomach with the shiny powder. "I guess both do work." She popped two mints in her mouth and then ran to RayAnne. "Ready."

"About time. I swear if I had to wait any longer, I might've keeled over." RayAnne parted the curtains and stepped out into the bar.

"You wish." Kyra smiled and strutted past RayAnne, swatting her ass on her way by. "Smile. The customers tip better when you do."

RayAnne rubbed her almost bare butt cheek. "If I smiled, my face might crack. Not sure I'd get too many tips then. Break a leg, baby." She gave Kyra a peck on the cheek and headed for the main stage.

They danced four nights a week at the Red Panther, a high-end gentleman's club in Hollywood. The club was clean, the bouncers were straight-tough, and the money was primo.

She and Kyra had been stripping/dancing as a team for almost twenty years, though thanks to their immortality freezing them in time, they both looked to be in their early twenties. And so far, it'd served both of them well.

Although they regularly changed up the choreography and music, they'd done the same routine for most of their partnership. They acted out a vampire scene: flashing fangs, nipping each other's skin, playing to their audience's most erotic and perverse fantasies.

Wednesday to Saturday nights, they ruled the roost as the feature act and raked in all the dough. It wasn't perfect, but it paid the bills and then some.

Thing was, none of the clientele had any idea they both were blood-sucking, fang-sporting, real deal, thing-of-nightmares vampires. Nothing worked better than hiding right out in the open.

Mario's voice rang out over the PA system from the DJ booth, drawing RayAnne's attention. "Red Panther friends, are you ready?" The crowd cheered, whistles sounding from the sea of dimly lit faces. "Here's what you've been waiting for. Ladies and Gents, put your hands together for our favorite vampires, Kyra Lee and RayAnne!"

She pulled her hood over her head and then climbed the three steps up to the main stage while another stripper collected her dollar bills from the floor around the pole. Kyra stepped off to the side. Puscifer's, *The Mission (M is for Milla Mix)* rang out, filling her mind and vibrating her chest with its strong beat.

With slow, measured steps, she walked the edge of the raised oblong stage, staring down at the horde of men surrounding the small tables covering almost every available section of carpet—sure to make eye contact with as many of them as possible.

She stopped downstage, legs spread apart, and raised her arms out to her sides before throwing her hips to one side with a harsh, exaggerated movement. The audience went wild, catcalling from their seats.

RayAnne scanned the main floor, absorbing every detail with her hawk-like vision, and as expected, it was void of the other strippers. No one would be paying for private dances while she and Kyra performed.

She spun on her platform, and as she strutted up stage, Kyra dropped down the metal pole. RayAnne circled behind her, and Kyra let go of the pole to face the audience. Again, the crowd cried out their appreciation.

Kyra's pleated plaid, schoolgirl skirt ended just above the rise of her full ass cheeks and sat low on her hips. Her equally little white shirt—unbuttoned and tied into a tight halter—accentuated her full breasts.

Just as she did damn near every night, RayAnne fell in love with her all over again.

Kyra backed up to the pole, her hands cupping both breasts, squeezing them together. RayAnne pressed her body against Kyra's, the metal pole between them. She ran the flat of her palms up Kyra's hips to her small waist while they both shifted from side to side in alternating directions.

Kyra sank down into a squatting position. Her bent legs spread wide. RayAnne raised one leg and draped it over Kyra's shoulder. Grabbing hold of the back of her partner's hair, RayAnne jerked Kyra's head to the side.

Kyra yanked from the hold, flipped her hair forward, and then licked RayAnne's inner thigh. RayAnne hissed, flashing fang, and the onlookers went nuts.

Kyra rose and strutted downstage, running her fingers through her long hair as she swayed her hips side to side. In an abrupt movement, RayAnne tore off her cloak and revealed her own costume—a red vinyl top with matching G-string—and then moved around Kyra and faced her.

Arching into a backbend, RayAnne locked eyes with the executive her partner mentioned earlier. Kyra ran her hands up RayAnne's body and over her breasts.

RayAnne welcomed the arousal erupting to life, spreading slow like molasses through her veins from Kyra's touch. She knew they looked as hot as she felt, yet he looked impassive...almost bored.

She broke eye contact with the businessman when Kyra ran her hands back down RayAnne's torso. RayAnne dropped from her arched position, her ass connecting with the cool stage floor—until Kyra went to her knees and pressed her pelvis between RayAnne's spread legs and ground against her, rubbing RayAnne's clit through her thin G-string.

The thumping beat of the song echoed around them, and they undulated together.

RayAnne rolled up, rising from her position on the floor. She stepped to the pole, gripped it and swung herself around and up, wind-milling her legs, splitting them wide when she spun.

On hands and knees, Kyra crawled to the end of the stage.

That's when the dollar bills began to fly, raining down around the stage—and they hadn't even exposed their breasts yet.

—————

Kyra

Kyra rose to her feet, rolling her body up in slow motion. She pivoted, swinging her head around, giving her back to the crowd.

With a tug on the knot holding her shirt together, she removed the small scrap of fabric, tossed it to the side and sprang into a backflip downstage.

Landing the trick, she continued, allowing her momentum to propel her into a split. She bounced and then bent forward, settling over her front leg, rolled over and back up again, facing the audience on the side of the stage. Rolling once more, she faced forward and settled in a Russian split, center stage.

Arching her back, she peered at RayAnne, who was working the pole. Kyra couldn't help but smile at her partner, who used her preternatural strength to suspend her body in ways many mortal strippers tried but could never do.

RayAnne pinched her nipples and scanned the crowd. Ten or so men had approached the stage, dollar bills in hand; lips arched into devious smirks. They were all just so cute.

The heady scent of lust and desire rolled off the crowd, filling her senses. Kyra couldn't help but giggle when she tugged on her nipples, causing even more eyes to glaze over in sexual hunger.

She flipped onto her hands and knees and slid over to the edge of the stage. With an arch in her back, she bounced her ass, her full butt cheeks shifting in time with the beat. She smoothed one hand up her thigh to her hip and then delivered a slap to one cheek.

One brave gentleman approached, a dollar in hand. Kyra licked one fang, smiled and then raised the side of her skirt, allowing him to slip the bill beneath the strap of her G-string. She winked at him and blew him a kiss before moving to the other side to collect from the men waiting there for her.

Kyra giggled and moved back to center stage. This was like taking candy from a baby. She shed her skirt and then turned and strolled to the pole.

RayAnne spun until she reached the bottom.

Kyra gripped the pole in one hand and hopped up, circling the pole above where RayAnne spun. Gripping the pipe between her thighs, she hung upside down, parallel to the bar.

RayAnne dismounted and stood in front of her.

Still upside-down, Kyra gripped RayAnne's thighs.

RayAnne wrapped her arms around Kyra's waist.

RayAnne backbended, and Kyra moved with her, rolling forward over the top of her. They flipped twice more, keeping their bodies together, before hitting the end of the stage.

When they separated, Kyra unhooked RayAnne's top, tossed it aside, and then cupped her partner's breasts in her palms, massaging them before tweaking and pulling on her nipples.

RayAnne leaned back against Kyra, undulating her petite frame against Kyra's taller one. She wrapped an arm around RayAnne's waist, bent them forward, then arched them back, their bodies moving in unison.

Kyra scraped a fang over RayAnne's shoulder, drawing a thin line of blood. As she did, she caught the gaze of the arrogant businessman. He never approached the stage. Always stayed in his seat at the same table, positioned in the corner of the main floor.

Kyra licked over the small scratch she'd made on RayAnne's skin.

He quirked one brow and then pursed his lips when Kyra licked her fang.

He'd propositioned her three times this week already. It was a kind of record for him, considering his proposition average was usually only once a week.

She always turned him down, and still, he was in the club every night she and RayAnne worked. He sipped his drink, paid for many private lap dances from her, and watched them —intent clear in his eyes—as they performed their show.

Just the sight of him turned her on, though damn if she knew why.

RayAnne gripped her hair, spinning Kyra around by her long locks and bringing her back to the moment and the fact they had a routine to finish.

Kyra linked arms with her and swung RayAnne back around, her partner using the momentum to fan her legs in the air before she got her feet back on the ground.

Yanking her back against her body, Kyra bent her head and scraped her fangs over her other shoulder, drawing blood from both thin gashes she created.

Dollar bills rained down around them. The distinct sound of the money flitting through the air wrapped around her, making her hungry for both sex and blood.

It was a melody like nothing she'd ever heard in the fifty

years she'd inhabited the earth as a human and now a vampire.

She and RayAnne moved to the pole. Kyra climbed to the top and then hung upside down in a spin, one leg locking her tight, the other extended to the side.

RayAnne took her position lower down, the pole wedged between a thigh and arm as she spun in aerial acrobatics.

Both shifted, linking their legs together around the pole, as they arched in opposite time, spinning and spinning. When they dropped to the floor, RayAnne grabbed Kyra's hair and forced her to her knees.

RayAnne stepped forward, bent over and reached between her legs.

Kyra clasped RayAnne's hands and slid on her side between her parted legs.

RayAnne flipped forward over Kyra's body and into a split.

Kyra crawled to RayAnne, gripped her face and kissed her.

The crowd roared.

They got to their feet, their bodies in an erotic embrace, and gazed over the audience, hissing, flashing fangs. RayAnne licked over one of Kyra's exposed breasts and then bit down, sinking her fangs into the tender flesh.

Kyra let out a yell, tossing her head back in mock pain.

The dollars flew again. RayAnne released her and pivoted away.

Kyra sank to her knees, her breast dripping blood down her stomach. She crawled along the edge of the stage, and patrons lined up to slip dollars into her G-string.

RayAnne had gone to work the pole one last time before the song ended, and their performance was over.

Kyra posed on hands and knees center stage, arching and rolling her hips. RayAnne dismounted and walked to her.

Kyra rolled to her back, her head at RayAnne's feet and

raised her legs in the air, clapping the sides of her platform heels together. She yanked Kyra down above her, then rolled and flipped them to face the audience.

She paused a moment, pressed against RayAnne's back and scanned the crowd. Locking gazes with their biggest fan in the corner, arousal blazed through Kyra and arrowed straight to her clit.

Though it was part of the act, lust was in charge. Kyra jerked RayAnne's head to the side and sank her fangs into her neck.

The final beats of the song approached. Kyra released RayAnne's throat and let the blood flow down her chest. She smeared it farther, spreading it down to RayAnne's stomach as her partner followed the path Kyra made with her palms, rocking her hips in time with Kyra's.

The entire audience was on their feet when the song ended, cheers echoing throughout the club. RayAnne stood and took a bow.

Then, it was Kyra's turn. The crowd clapped, cheered and tossed more money on the stage. Kyra beamed, excitement beating through her.

She couldn't help it. She felt like some sort of beauty queen or movie star, something she'd never been or ever would be. But the fantasy was good, just the same.

Chapter Two

RayAnne

RAYANNE SLIPPED OFF her shoes and took a seat at the dressing table. "How much?"

Kyra sat at the other table, counting the cash she'd pulled off the stage. "Three hundred, twenty-two."

"That's it?" RayAnne pulled off one set of false eyelashes and then the other and blinked, clearing her vision. "Count it again."

"Ooohkay. But I think I got it right the first time." Kyra rolled her eyes and began counting the money again.

RayAnne figured they'd brought in at least four, maybe even four-fifty. Three wasn't satisfactory in her book. She pulled a wipe out of the plastic dispenser and swiped down her chest.

"Three hundred, twenty-two." Kyra smiled. "Just like I said the first time."

RayAnne sighed. "We need to work out a new routine this week." Apparently, the current one wasn't working as well as many of their others.

"Okay. What theme this time?"

10

"I'm not sure. I'll have to give it some thought." RayAnne finished the blood cleanup and then stripped off her G-string. Donning a new outfit, she turned to Kyra. "We need to work the floor tonight. You coming?"

"Yeah." She shrugged, inspecting her nails. "I guess."

"Well, paste on that pretty smile of yours and go charm your favorite businessman." RayAnne pulled a brush through her dark hair.

Kyra gasped. "He's so not my favorite businessman. He could be if you let me bring him home for playtime, but you won't."

"Why? So you can hear him say, 'you're welcome,' after you fuck him?" RayAnne snorted a laugh.

"Ugh, I know, right?" She tugged on a new G-string, silver with pink stars. "There's just something about how he looks at us. Like he's got some sort of secret, and he's only going to tell us if we ask in just the right way." Kyra giggled. "Bet he's a freak."

"Bet he takes it up the ass." RayAnne applied a new coat of lip gloss.

Kyra burst into a fit of giggles. "Oh my word, do you think? All buttoned up, suit and tie. And the cowboy boots. Let's not forget the boots."

"Especially because of the boots."

Kyra's face lit up like fireworks on the Fourth of July, and she clapped her hands. "Can we? Oh my goodness, can we take him home tonight? I've been a really good girl since the last time. Please? And it's been forever. Pleaaaase, RayAnne?"

RayAnne glanced at her lover; the excitement palpitated off of her in waves she could practically see. She supposed Kyra was right; she *had* been behaving. Last time they took a customer home, Kyra had gotten a little carried away and almost broke him. Literally.

Since that night, RayAnne had to impose a rule: no more customers, at least not for a while. It'd been months, though, and although the silver-haired executive didn't particularly appeal to her, he turned Kyra's knobs. And RayAnne was horny, so fuck it. Why not?

She smiled. "If he asks again tonight, then okay. But, no propositioning him. Got me?"

"Yes!" Kyra bounced, her large breasts bouncing with her.

"All right, let's get out there and make up what we didn't earn during our act. Fucking cheap bastards. I hate doing lap dances. If I must do them, I'm going to make them worth my while. They'll pay in dollars, or I'll sneak a few sips of blood. Either way works for me."

Kyra was still smiling from ear to ear when they made their way out to the main floor. She made a beeline for the businessman, as RayAnne figured she might.

God help that child. She was a glutton. RayAnne knew the guy was the definition of arrogant, and it rather made her loathe being around him.

Mortals were such dicks at times.

Provided he asked, she looked forward to taking him down a peg or ten.

———

Kyra

Kyra approached her target in hopes he'd proposition her just one more time.

She and RayAnne didn't usually work the floor after their performances, so she was happy to see he was still seated in his usual spot.

He was good for at least a few lap dances from her tonight. At least she could grind all over his cock through his thin dress pants and get him nice and hard and then draw an orgasm out of him he'd never forget.

Puscifer's *Rev 22:20* came on, and Kyra scanned the crowd

for RayAnne. The DJ knew she was partial to this band and was most likely trying to make her night a little better.

Kyra spotted her—perched on a customer's thighs, her G-string-covered pussy right in his face. RayAnne undulated her body in time with the beat of the song. Hot. Very hot.

Turning her attention back to the businessman, Kyra caught his gaze, adjusted her bra top, and smoothed her palms over her breasts.

He quirked an eyebrow, took a sip of his drink, and then nodded for her to come over.

"Glad to see you still here. Would you like another dance?" She bent forward, resting her hands on his thighs.

He tilted his head to the side and glanced down at her cleavage. "Why are you still here?"

Okay, maybe he wanted to talk instead. "We decided to stay a little late tonight."

"Have a seat." He motioned to the empty chair next to his. "Not enough money on the set tonight?"

Kyra frowned but took the seat next to him. "That's kinda a rude question, isn't it?"

"See it how you wish. Rude or not, it's an accurate question."

"I guess." She looked around, suddenly wanting to be anywhere but near him now. She didn't mind direct people, but rude was a totally different story.

"Let me get you a drink." He waved the waitress over. "What would you like?"

"I'll have a glass of champagne. The Dom Rose, please?" She smiled at the waitress. May as well order the top-shelf stuff and ensure the waitress got a big tip as a result.

"Expensive taste." He sipped his drink.

"Not something you expected from a stripper?"

"You don't seem like the champagne type."

"Oh, I'm all champagne and bubbles." She crossed her legs. "It's RayAnne who prefers things a bit more serious."

"I see. Are those your real names?"

"Yes, actually, they are." Her drink arrived, and she smiled at him, raising her glass in toast. "What's your name?"

"Dana Richards. What are we drinking to?"

"Nice to meet you, Dana Richards. We're drinking to your next proposition, of course." She winked and sipped from the glass.

He looked a bit confused before he raised his drink to his lips and took a sip. For whatever reason, the idea she'd stumped him made her all giddy inside—more than usual.

"What is it you believe I'll be proposing?"

"You seem like a very smart man. An executive, right? An important one?" She let her eyes widen, exaggerating her interest in him. "I've seen several articles in the paper about you."

He chuckled. "Yes, Kyra. I'm an executive, and I guess you could say an important one. Why do you ask?"

"Honestly, I think it's fascinating. I don't think I could do it personally, though. You know, work a day job. In an office somewhere. Seems like a lot of rules to follow." She scrunched up her nose.

"It is a lot of responsibility, yes. I imagine you don't like rules."

"Not particularly."

"I'm curious. What happens when there are rules imposed on you?" He smoothed his hand down the back of his salt-and-pepper hair—more salt than pepper.

"I break them, of course." She smiled and then took a sip of her champagne.

"I bet you do." He pursed his lips and cocked his head to the side. "What if *you* get to make the rules?"

"I don't." She shrugged. "RayAnne makes the rules."

"I see. And you break them." He sipped his drink.

"Exactly." She nodded with a grin.

"Is that what you're doing now, breaking rules?"

"How do you mean?" Where was he going with this?

"By sitting here, talking to me. Shouldn't you be attending to the other customers?"

"Am I not attending to you?"

"Just checking."

She giggled. "But you haven't asked me for a dance yet."

"What happens if I don't ask you for a dance? Will you be breaking rules then?"

"Yes… but…"

"You're welcome."

Ugh, he was so strange. She frowned and narrowed her eyes. And maybe a little twisted, too. RayAnne was probably right; he probably did take it up the ass. "You always say that. Why?"

"It's polite." He grinned.

"But I didn't thank you for anything."

"Sure you did."

"Oookay. If you say so."

"A lot of people thank me for many things and don't know it. Drink your champagne, then you can dance for me."

"Are you going to tell me 'you're welcome' if I do?"

"If you earn it."

She shook her head and took a long swallow of her drink. Scanning the crowd, she spotted RayAnne talking to one of the bouncers.

RayAnne caught Kyra's eyes and nodded. A small smile curved Kyra's lips at her partner's way of checking on her to be sure she was okay. Kyra returned the nod and then gazed back at Dana.

Strange name for a strange man, but she supposed it fit. She took in his profile while he watched one of the dancers up on stage. He wasn't a very big man, as far as bulk and height. But he always wore his suits quite well. And Kyra liked that about him.

"Would you like a private one this time?"

He looked at her. "Depends. What do I get for a private one?"

Kyra stood and then straddled his hips. She smoothed her fingertips down his burgundy print tie. "What would you like?"

He let out a soft breath, his eyes going heavy behind his glasses. "You know what I want."

She leaned forward, brushing the tip of her nose over his ear. "Ask again." She kept her words to a whisper, letting her breath feather over his skin. "Ask again, and this time, I'll say yes." He shuddered, and a bolt of satisfaction shot through her.

She was getting to him with almost no effort. Points for her.

"I'd prefer a private dance, but only if it's outside of the club."

She pulled away and gazed at him. "Done. One thing though—a thousand for the night."

His eyes went wide. "Do I look like a man who would pay for such a thing?"

"Not at all." She rolled her hips, and he sucked in a breath. "Do I look like a woman who takes her customer home and fucks him until he doesn't know his own name?"

"Jesus Christ. You do." He tilted his head to the side. "The thought of what you can do with that body and mouth of yours is damn near enough to make me pay to find out."

"We're worth it." She licked her lips.

"We're?"

"Yep, me and RayAnne. You get two for the price of one."

"Fuck me." He scrubbed his hand over his mouth.

"Oh, I intend to do just that. Meet us out back in the alley in thirty minutes."

"Done."

Chapter Three

RayAnne

"WHERE IS HE?" RayAnne stubbed out her cigarette.

"He'll be here." Kyra picked at her nail polish. "Ugh, I need to redo these."

"He better be. We're losing money right now." She crossed her arms over her chest.

"Yeah, but if he shows, think how much we'll be making." Kyra smiled. Her full lips practically begged to be kissed.

RayAnne couldn't stand it anymore. She'd gotten so amped up during their routine she needed to take the edge off. She pulled Kyra close and cupped one of her full breasts in her palm. "You were such a fucking tease tonight on that stage."

Kyra moaned. "Yeah? I scented your arousal while I was grinding against you."

"I'm so fucking you good and hard tonight." RayAnne pulled her down for a hard kiss; her fangs grazed Kyra's bottom lip, earning her a small taste of the tangy, sweet blood she brought forth. "So fucking sweet. Just as sweet as your pussy tastes."

Kyra rubbed against her, whimpering like a little kitten, as a set of headlights illuminated the back alleyway.

"He showed!" Kyra let out a squeal, pulled away from RayAnne and moved toward his black BMW.

He rolled the window down and peered out at them. "You ladies need a ride?"

"Absofuckinglutely!" Kyra opened the passenger door.

RayAnne slid into the back. When they were all closed inside the car, she stuck her palm out between the two front seats. "Money."

"I don't pay for a service until I've received said service."

Kyra pouted. "But—"

"I'll give you half now and half when we're done, and, as you promised," he grinned, his eyes crinkling at the corners, "I no longer remember my name."

RayAnne gritted her teeth and then forced a smile. "Deal." She sat back. "Kyra, give him our address so he can add it to the fancy GPS he's got in the dash."

"Wouldn't a hotel be preferable?" He glanced over his shoulder at her.

"I prefer to have my things."

He held RayAnne's eyes for what felt like forever before he looked away and entered the address Kyra dictated to him. "All right. Your place it is."

RayAnne focused on the passing buildings and then the lights of the city in the distance as they made their way into the hills of Glendale.

"Nice neighborhood. I'm impressed." He turned onto their street.

"Not what you expected?"

"I have to admit, no." He glanced at her in the mirror and then pulled into their driveway.

"I'll get the garage." Kyra hopped out.

"Pull in the garage, please." RayAnne grabbed her bag.

"Why?" He glanced over his shoulder at her.

"Are you going to be this combative all night?" She leaned forward.

"Are you going to be this pushy?"

RayAnne tilted her head to the side and pursed her lips. He was better off learning the rules now. "Yes."

"A woman who likes to be in charge. Not the first time I've come across that, won't be the last." He pulled forward into their garage. "And certainly nothing I can't handle."

"Then I guess you'll be just fine. Kyra will walk you inside and get you a drink. I'll get my things prepared." RayAnne opened the door and stepped out.

"As you wish." He got out of the car and shut the door.

"Follow me, Dana. I know the way to heaven." Kyra grinned and linked her arm in his.

RayAnne made her way up to her bedroom, tossed her baseball cap on the bed and then stripped off her jeans and t-shirt.

Annoyance ricocheted through her. She didn't much like his arrogant attitude and definitely looked forward to teaching him a few lessons tonight.

After washing her hands, she ran her fingers through her hair and then pulled on a low-cut slip dress. She moved to the large chest at the foot of her bed. Lifting the lid, she sorted through the various items stored in there.

"Let's see…" RayAnne grabbed the blindfold, flogger, the wrist and ankle cuffs, two vibrators and the strap-on—oh, yes, if Mr. Dana Richards didn't already take it in the ass, he was going to tonight.

At the last second, she grabbed the lube. She wasn't that much of a sadist. She loaded up a bag with the toys and wandered downstairs to the private library—AKA the playroom.

After setting up the items on the sideboard against the

wall, she lit the many candles scattered throughout the room and then went in search of Kyra and their plaything for the night. She discovered them in the formal living room.

"Kyra, would you like to go change?"

Kyra stood. "I would." She smiled and shifted her hips from side to side. Kyra's excitement boiled over into the room, and pleasure replaced RayAnne's annoyance. RayAnne looked forward to expelling a good portion of that energy for Kyra throughout the night.

RayAnne watched Kyra walk by and then turned her focus back on him. "Are you enjoying your drink?"

"Yes, thank you." He crossed his leg over his knee. "You have a beautiful home."

"Thank you. I'm quite partial to it."

"Have you lived here long?"

"A few years." She moved to the wet bar and fixed herself a whiskey. They'd lived in this house for almost fifteen years, but there was no reason for him to know that. Especially because she still looked twenty-five. She walked toward him and took a seat across from him.

"You don't like me very much, do you?"

"I don't have to like you to fuck you."

"I thought it might be nice if we were friends." He sipped his drink.

She sighed. "Mr. Richards—"

"Please, call me Dana." He adjusted his tie.

"Fine. Dana, this is a business deal. Considering your high-profile position, I'm certain you're accustomed to handling business without being friends with your customers."

"Apples and oranges. I don't fuck my customers."

"Neither do I." RayAnne sipped her whiskey.

He frowned and leaned forward. "Then why am I here?"

She shrugged one shoulder. "Kyra likes you. And I like to make her happy."

"So basically, what you're telling me is, you'll tolerate me because Kyra likes me?"

"Yes." She swallowed the last of her drink.

"Why would you do that?"

"That's," she set her glass down, "none of your business."

"Look, I'm not interested in people doing things they don't want to do." He stood.

"Oh, please." She crossed one leg over the other, exposing a generous amount of thigh. "I know exactly how cutthroat you are. Dana Richards, the famous executive, would sell his own kin if it'd make him another hundred K. So why should it matter if I like you?"

His nostrils flared, and he frowned.

RayAnne tilted her head to the side. Mr. Arrogant just let his sensitive side slip out. How interesting.

He let out a sigh and sat back down. "I know what the papers say. Doesn't mean they're right. I might play hardball where business is concerned, but I'm not a prick."

She tucked a lock of hair behind her ear and raised her brows. "Fine. Regardless, my question is still valid. Does it matter?"

"I suppose if it doesn't to you, then it doesn't to me." He downed the last of his scotch.

"Then we're agreed. You can pay me half of the money now." She held out her hand.

He stared at her for a long time, like he'd done in the car, before pulling the billfold from inside his suit jacket pocket. He took out five one-hundred dollar bills and fanned them out on the end table between them. "You're welcome."

RayAnne tilted her chin forward and stared at him. She parted her lips, licked one fang, and scooped up the money. "I do believe you'll be thanking *me* later."

———

Kyra

KYRA RAN UPSTAIRS. She knew exactly how RayAnne wanted her to get ready. Kyra showered, washing away the glitter from her body and then smoothed her lavender lotion on every inch of her skin. When she was done, she put on her collar and nothing else.

Excitement pulsed through her, vibrating her limbs. She couldn't wait to taste Dana's blood. RayAnne's blood tasted like honeysuckle, sweet and smooth. There was nothing like the high that came from sampling that honeyed red liquid.

Plus, RayAnne was going to fuck the living shit out of her tonight, and Kyra couldn't wait for that either.

After she finished a light bit of makeup, she made her way downstairs to the playroom. RayAnne had already set everything up, lit all the candles and set the gas fireplace to blaze.

The overly large, tufted round leather ottoman sat waiting for her in the center of the room. Kyra crawled on it and positioned herself on her back, arms out to her sides, and waited.

"God, you're fucking beautiful."

Kyra opened her eyes to see RayAnne staring down at her. "Thank you, baby." She smiled.

RayAnne leaned forward and pressed a kiss to her lips.

Kyra opened, rolling her tongue over RayAnne's, and moaned into her mouth. Lust rose fast, like a summer storm in her belly, and her fangs lengthened.

RayAnne pinched both of Kyra's nipples, tugging them and rolling them between her fingertips.

Kyra arched off the ottoman.

Abruptly, RayAnne broke the kiss.

Kyra wanted to pull her close, feel her lips on hers again, but knew better than to move her arms and hands from the open position they rested in.

She glanced over and saw Dana in the doorway. Eyes

wide, his focus clearly centered on her. Kyra wondered if he'd ever been with two women before.

She doubted it but knew for damn sure he'd never been with one, much less two, vampires.

Chapter Four

RayAnne

"I'll allow you to watch first. Have a seat over there." RayAnne used the black and red leather flogger she'd picked up to point at the chair set off to the side of the fireplace.

"Gladly." Dana moved to the seat, removed his jacket and folded it over the back of the chair before sitting down. "You've left your fangs in, I see."

"They're permanent." RayAnne turned up the volume a few more notches on the iPod deck with the remote and turned back to Kyra.

She gazed down at her naked form. Her pale skin glowed in the light of the fire and candles. Her long blonde hair with its pink and black streaks fanned out like a halo around her head.

She was a glorious sight, and RayAnne intended to make her even more so before the night was through.

Fiona Apple's *Slow Like Honey* played in the background, and RayAnne twirled the flogger in her hand.

"Interesting." He crossed one leg over the other. "I guess if that's your thing."

"Better to bite you with." Kyra winked at him.

"We'll see about the biting." He cleared his throat.

There'd be plenty of biting—and drinking of his blood. RayAnne was sure he'd love every moment of it, too. Just as each human they'd taken home to play with had.

"We certainly will." RayAnne returned her attention to Kyra. "Raise your hands above your head, love."

Kyra complied with the direction, and her lips split into a small smile.

Pleased with how submissive Kyra always was when it was playtime, RayAnne nodded. She circled the ottoman to the right, squared her shoulders, and planted her feet firmly beneath her.

Careful to keep her body straight, she gripped the strands of the leather flogger in one hand as she raised it in the air and then dropped the strips across Kyra's breasts, landing her mark with perfect precision.

Immediately, Kyra arched her back, and the small sigh from her lips that followed it filled RayAnne's ears. She struck again, the same spot, but with a little more force.

Kyra moaned, and her pale nipples tightened into firm peaks. Satisfaction raced through RayAnne at Kyra's physical and emotional response.

Dana cursed low from the corner, the sound birthing a pool of lust in RayAnne's stomach. She picked up the pace, striking Kyra's breasts with a speed and accuracy no mortal could.

Kyra moaned and writhed, her pale skin rising to a pale pink shade as the nerve endings jumped to life with each lash of the flogger.

Pleased and thoroughly aroused by her work, RayAnne shifted her stance and struck again, slapping higher on Kyra's chest. She repeated the motion over and over, Kyra moaning and whimpering the whole time until RayAnne was once again satisfied with the color she'd brought to the surface.

By the time she'd finished, Kyra's eyes had glossed over, her breath coming out in harsh pants. Desire sparked and popped through RayAnne like an electrical circuit on overload when she gazed down at Kyra's beautiful body.

RayAnne glanced over at Dana. Utterly transfixed, his breaths sawed in and out, and sweat dotted his forehead. RayAnne's fangs lengthened in anticipation of how hot his blood would taste on her tongue.

"Come here." She extended her hand. His gaze darted to her and then back to Kyra before he rose and walked to her. "Do you like what you see laid out before you?"

"Who wouldn't?" He smoothed his palm over his mouth. "I like it very much."

She circled behind him, smoothing her hand over his ass, and then bent to his ear. "Do you think she's beautiful?"

"Extremely."

RayAnne ran a finger down the side of his neck. His pulse beat hard and fast, the blood just below the surface, a tantalizing bite away. "Do you want to fuck her?"

He visibly shivered. "Again, who wouldn't?"

RayAnne pinched his chin between her finger and thumb and jerked his head in her direction. "A simple yes or no is expected."

He stared at her with defiance in his eyes.

Would he fall in line or fight her? She wasn't sure.

After a moment, he exhaled and then answered. "Yes."

"Very good. Now, remove your shirt, kneel before her, and show me how well you can work that smart tongue of yours on her cunt."

Again, she wasn't certain he'd obey, but really, what man wouldn't in his position? He removed his glasses and then stripped off his shirt, revealing a surprisingly toned chest, and dropped down in front of Kyra.

He looked up at RayAnne as if making sure he was free to proceed.

How interesting.

She nodded, blinking her eyes in a slow show of acknowledgment. "Spread your legs for your businessman, Kyra."

She did as RayAnne instructed, her movements unhurried, still dazed from the rush of endorphins blanketing her senses.

Dana smoothed his palms down the inside of Kyra's thighs and then ran them back up again. He spread the lips of her perfect pussy, bent his head and gave one long lick from ass to clit.

Kyra's moan had RayAnne clenching her thighs together. She set her stance behind him, gripped the strands of the flogger, and released it across his upper back.

Dana let out a growl, but rather than stopping his task, as RayAnne thought he might, he grabbed hold of Kyra's hips and buried his face in her pussy with fervor.

Sweet heaven, this night would be one to remember for a long time.

————

Kyra

PLEASURE BOOMERANGED through Kyra's limbs as Dana licked and sucked at her cunt like a starving man.

With each lap of his tongue, he drove her toward orgasm.

RayAnne lashed at his back with the flogger. Each time she landed a blow, the leather straps slapping against his skin, he growled against her pussy, sending vibrations deep inside her.

Her orgasm was edging closer. She clenched her fists and caught RayAnne's gaze.

"Not yet, love. Hold on to that sweet climax of yours." RayAnne lashed Dana's back.

He jerked away, arching his back. "Fuck!"

"Oh? Too much for you?"

He glared at RayAnne, his nostrils flaring with his heavy breath.

"Shhh. It's okay." Kyra sat up. He looked back at her, and she kissed him.

The taste of her honey flowed into her mouth from his lips and tongue, and she let out a whimper.

Dana tangled his fingers in her hair, and Kyra ran her nails down his chest.

"You taste so fucking divine. I've never tasted a pussy so good in my life." He licked his lips.

"I know." She smiled, lay back down, and then pushed his head between her legs.

Damn right, she was sweet. Every inch of her skin, mouth and cunt tasted like cotton-candy.

RayAnne's pussy tasted like honeysuckle, like her blood. It was one of the perks that came along with their vampiric nature—endless beauty, perfect skin, bodies and yes, even their taste. Taste was unique to each vampire, though, like the color of someone's eyes or hair.

The first time Kyra sucked a vampire's cock, she thought she might up and die (funny since she was already dead) because his cum tasted like marshmallow ambrosia with bananas and coconut.

RayAnne gave one more lash to his back and then bent behind him and licked over his skin.

Transfixed, Kyra held RayAnne's gaze as her tongue snaked out and over his neck and shoulder, the tips of her fangs visible each time she opened her mouth.

The sight made Kyra's own fangs ache to sink into warm, giving flesh.

Dana penetrated her core with two fingers and sucked her clit.

Kyra's climax came rushing to the surface, and she rocked

her pelvis, taking his fingers deeper. Devil in hell, she was going to come so hard when RayAnne finally allowed her to.

"Let me see what you have for us." RayAnne came around to his side and undid his dress pants.

Kyra craned her neck to the side, trying to get a view of what lay in wait beneath his boxers.

Then another sensation hit home with such force she almost screamed. Dana penetrated her ass with two fingers slick with her juices and latched onto her clit, sucking so hard she saw stars.

She raised her head and blinked, clearing her vision, barely able to hold her orgasm at bay.

RayAnne was at Dana's ear, her lips moving, saying things Kyra couldn't hear, her arm shifting up and down, stroking his cock.

Kyra's lust ratcheted up another ten notches, breaching her mental barriers, and she cried out, rolling her hips in time with the thrust of his fingers and the shift of RayAnne's arm.

Oh, fuck, she was going to come without permission. There was almost no way she could stop it now.

Chapter Five

RayAnne

RayAnne was pleasantly surprised at what Dana was hiding inside his boxers. Not overly long, but definitely thick. His cock curved up to his belly and was rock-motherfucking-hard.

Smooth skin, void of any pubic hair. Yes, definitely a pleasant surprise. She'd enjoy sucking him later. And then watching Kyra suck him, too.

RayAnne groaned, and her clit pulsed. Kyra had the most sensual lips, and the thought of them wrapped tight around his thick shaft was almost enough to make RayAnne sink her fangs into his shoulder.

Kyra let out a high-pitched moan.

RayAnne knew what that sound meant. Her lover was about to come. But RayAnne wasn't ready to let her…yet.

She pulled away from Dana and rounded the ottoman to where Kyra's head lay. "You want to come, don't you, lover?"

"God, yes! Please?"

RayAnne pulled her slip dress over her head, dropped it to the floor and climbed onto the ottoman. She straddled Kyra's head and bent forward over her body, coming face to face with Dana—her pussy right above Kyra's mouth. "Lick me, and I'll let you come."

"Holy fuck." Dana looked up, eyes as wide as silver dollars.

RayAnne gripped him by the back of the head and kissed him. Kyra's sweet cotton-candy flavor slid into her mouth when his tongue stroked over hers. At the same time, Kyra sucked RayAnne's clit between her lips.

RayAnne tilted her pelvis forward and moaned into his mouth. He kissed about as good as any immortal she'd played with, but it lit a fire inside her she hadn't expected.

Fucking hell, for whatever reason, the situation had gone from what she thought was going to be an average fuck session to an overload of oh-my-fucking-god-if-I-don't-come-I'm-going-to-die session.

The music—Type O Negative's, *Love You To Death*—echoed around them, mingling with their sighs and moans.

The scent of Kyra's and her arousal mixed with the musk of Dana's precum permeated her senses, and her body shook with the sexual energy filling the room.

Kyra's tongue flicked RayAnne's clit, and she groaned into Dana's mouth. As her head spun, she gave herself over to the moment.

Oh, yes, all three of them would be fucked hard and rough tonight. There would be many orgasms as a result. And this once refined executive would definitely not remember his name by the time she and Kyra had their fill of him.

She tore from the kiss and shoved his face back between her lover's spread thighs, and then ground her pussy against Kyra's mouth.

Kyra's moans vibrated through RayAnne's core, and her breath punched out of her in a heavy rush.

Dana groaned, staring up at her while he sucked Kyra's

clit. RayAnne pinched her nipples and licked a fang, on the verge of her own orgasm. "Make her come. Now."

The little whimpers and moans coming from Kyra bled into a muffled scream, and she slid her fangs into RayAnne's folds, sucking her clit deep into her mouth.

Kyra's orgasm broke free, and her hips jerked off the leather cushion.

RayAnne bent forward and held his head against Kyra's cunt.

Dana growled, his eyes rolling to the back of his head before he closed them.

The erotic penetration of Kyra's fangs, the sensations of her vibrating tongue on RayAnne's clit, took RayAnne over the edge. Her climax hit like a tornado, sweeping her away until she thought she might break into a million tiny shards of herself.

With shaky legs, she rose off Kyra and moved to Dana's side. He was still lapping at her lover's folds, moaning as he did so.

Kyra lay limp, her eyes closed, drawing in breath after breath. They didn't actually need to breathe, but in certain situations, exceptional sexual release being one of them, the body took over and did what it was born to do.

RayAnne smiled and ran her fingers through Dana's hair. She gripped the soft strands and jerked his head back from Kyra's pussy.

He gazed up at her, a stupefied look in his eyes, and licked his lips. "What about you? Did you come too?"

He shook his head. "No."

Interesting. He was chock-full of surprises. She glanced down at his fully erect penis. The bulbous head flushed red from all the blood flow. Flow she could almost hear. "You're welcome."

His eyes widened for a moment before he closed them and swallowed, his Adam's apple bobbing with the action.

"Kyra, get up, lover. I think the gentleman needs to lie down."

———

Kyra

KYRA HADN'T EXPECTED Dana to be so good with his tongue and fingers. And when RayAnne straddled her face, her sweet honeysuckle-flavored cunt against her tongue, Kyra literally lost her mind.

It was one hell of a climax, and the aftershocks were still rippling through her.

Kyra rubbed her eyes, smiled and rolled off the ottoman. "Gladly."

RayAnne dropped to her knees and wrapped her hand around his cock. Dana thrust his hips forward, driving his cock through RayAnne's fist.

Kyra moved to his other side and kissed him. Dearest vampire gods, his tongue…she moaned, desire spiking again. His tongue still carried her flavor mixed with something she couldn't quite make out but liked a whole lot.

Kyra ran her hand down his chest, scraping her nails along his soft skin. His body went rigid, and Kyra glanced down.

RayAnne held the head of his cock in her fist. She was squeezing, the outside of her fingers coated with a bit of ejaculate.

Unable to resist, Kyra bent and licked over RayAnne's fingers.

"There you go, lover. Clean that up for me." Then RayAnne spoke over his loud cries. "Good boy. You stopped. So close, I know. Not yet, though. Not until I say." She let out a sinister laugh.

Kyra swallowed his cum, and her pussy clenched in need.

She wanted to suck him into her mouth and feel him come down the back of her throat. Then she wanted to fuck him.

"I'm not a boy." He gasped. "Jesus Christ, you're killing me."

"Not yet, I'm not." RayAnne pulled her hand away and urged him onto the ottoman. When he was settled on his back, RayAnne moved to the sideboard and grabbed the wrist cuffs. "Raise your hands above your head."

"I don't—"

"Yes, you do. Trust me, you just don't know it yet. Now, do as I say."

He raised his hands. "This is nuts. You're nuts! Shouldn't there be a safe word or something?"

How cute. Kyra giggled. "No, we're not silly. And a safe word? If you think you're going to need one. Sure."

He glanced down at her. "Do *you* think I'm going to need one?"

"If anything's for certain, you won't want one." She ran her fingertips up his parted thighs, her mouth watering at the sight of his cock bobbing against his belly.

"You're welcome." RayAnne fastened a cuff on each of his wrists and then linked them together.

Dana chuckled and started to object again, but then quieted when RayAnne bent and kissed him.

Kyra focused on his hard shaft, seeing the blood flow through the thick vein that ran along it. A whimper bubbled up out of her in anticipation of how sweet that hot blood might taste.

She ran her nail along the vein, smiling as his cock twitched and his stomach tightened in response. She giggled again and gazed over his body with wide eyes.

Like a kid in a candy store, she wanted to eat every bit of him up, but was unable to decide where to start.

"Would you like to suck his cock, lover?"

She smiled at RayAnne. "Very much so, yes."

RayAnne knelt at his head and bent close to his ear. "Are you ready for Kyra to suck you?"

"Please, yes." He sucked in a breath.

RayAnne nipped his earlobe and, instead of moving away, stayed close to him, her palms spread out on his chest. Kyra held her gaze and leaned between his parted thighs and licked his tight sac.

"Fuck!" He jerked his hips forward.

"Stay still." RayAnne dug her nails into his chest.

Panting, he looked up and then nodded.

Kyra grinned and stroked her tongue over his balls and sucked each globe, careful to not scrape the tender skin with her fangs.

There'd be plenty of time for biting soon enough. The clean taste and scent of him raced through her, stoking the fire of lust burning in her veins to an inferno.

Moving higher, she licked a line up his shaft to the head, cradling the length gently in her palm. Kyra climbed onto the tufted surface and knelt between his legs. With her eyes locked on his face, she snaked out her tongue and licked the slit at the crown, tasting the salty goodness oozing from the tip.

She couldn't help the moan that erupted from her, mirroring the one that spilled from him as well.

She smiled, holding his gaze, and then curled her tongue around the rim. Satisfaction spread through her like molasses. Kyra loved sucking dick.

When she had a lover, she made a point, as soon as the sun was down, to be on her knees, ready and willing. The sounds coming out of Dana, the little whimpers, moans and sharp inhalations of breath, spurred her on.

Kyra pressed her mouth to the head and then, with slow, deliberate movement, parted her lips, sliding him between them until he bumped the back of her throat.

She held him there, swallowing, relaxing her throat, and losing herself in the cadence of his pulse. With no need to breathe, she could hold him there all night if she wanted, sucking and reveling in every twitch and jerk of his prick.

She hummed for several seconds and then dragged her mouth back to the head. With his length held tight in her palm, she stroked him from base to tip and watched in awe while another bead of pre-cum formed at the slit. She spread it over the head with her thumb and then followed her hand back down to the base with her mouth.

"Oh, God! Killing me. Your mouth is…Jesus. It's incredible." He licked his lips.

"She is quite talented." RayAnne tilted his head to the side and pressed her lips to his neck.

Kyra knew RayAnne sucked at the thick vein there, probing it with her tongue and the tip of her fangs. She'd be the first to break skin, and most likely right when he exploded, spurting down Kyra's throat.

The thought plowed through her like a freight train, and her clit pulsed. In answer, she sucked him harder, drawing him in and out of her mouth, twisting her palm along the shaft with each pass.

His moans grew louder, his breath faster. His cock twitched in her mouth, and another drop of precum coated her tongue. He'd gone mindless, his hips moving in time with her.

"Please?" A heavy mask of strain blanketed his face.

She glanced at her partner and nodded. RayAnne nodded back, giving Kyra permission, and she took him to the back of her throat and hummed, holding him there and swallowing with her tongue flat against his shaft.

"Come for her, Dana. Come now."

"*Fuuuuckkk!* God, yes!" His hips shot up off the ottoman.

Kyra looked up to see RayAnne pierce his neck with her

fangs, and as a result, Kyra orgasmed—without even touching herself.

At the same time, Dana's climax hit hard and fast, his cock pulsing in her mouth. Hot spurts jetted into the back of her throat.

Kyra closed her eyes and swallowed, sucking every drop he gave her.

Chapter Six

RayAnne

DANA'S BLOOD flowed fast and hot into RayAnne's mouth, and she closed her eyes and moaned. He tasted like sweet sangria mixed with a hint of the scotch he always drank.

When she opened her eyes, she focused on Kyra, who was still working him, his cock buried deep in her mouth as he moaned and writhed beneath her, caught up in the storm of his climax.

The bite she'd just given—thanks to the venom-like substance she excreted from her fangs—was painless. Although he was so immersed in the feel of Kyra's mouth and his orgasm, RayAnne doubted he would've noticed anyway.

The venom served another purpose, too. It lowered inhibitions and acted as an aphrodisiac, though he'd remain alert enough to object if he really wasn't down with anything they wanted to do with him. Dana could say no if he chose to.

Kyra drew her mouth off his length and then lapped at the head.

Dana whimpered, and another rope of semen spurted from his dick.

Kyra smiled and licked the head. The sight of her pink tongue spurred RayAnne's desire higher. She withdrew her fangs and licked over the small puncture wounds, sealing them closed.

Dana's body was lax, his eyes closed, a look of sheer contentment blanketing his features.

She moved to the sideboard and secured the strap-on harness around her hips, then grabbed the bottle of lube and moved back to the ottoman.

"Straddle his face, Kyra. I'm going to fuck you while he sucks your clit for me."

Clapping her hands, Kyra squealed and jumped off the ottoman. She bent over Dana's head and tapped his cheek. "Ready, honey?"

"Mmhmm." He turned his head, a sly smile curving his lips, and then pressed them to her palm in a sleepy kiss. Perfect.

Kyra bent closer and licked at his lips, coaxing his mouth open. When he complied, she slanted her mouth over his and kissed him.

Watching the kiss, RayAnne's pussy ached, needing to be filled, and her clit throbbed. She'd let him fuck her tonight for sure.

She didn't always let the men they brought home have intercourse with her. Most times, she was satisfied watching Kyra get fucked, and then, in turn, having Kyra eat her pussy, bringing her to beautiful climax every time.

But tonight, without a doubt, she wanted a cock inside her. She wanted his cock inside her.

RayAnne smoothed her hand down the curve of Kyra's perfect ass and then slid her fingers between her thighs through her soft folds.

Her girl was nice and wet, as expected.

Kyra moaned at the contact and arched her back, raising her ass to RayAnne.

Such a greedy little slut! And RayAnne loved every fucking inch of her for it, but still… "Naughty girl." She slapped one of Kyra's ass cheeks, and the sharp sound echoed around them. "You know I'll take this ass if I want it. Whenever I want it. Now, quit dilly-dallying and do as I told you to."

"Yes, baby." Kyra moved to Dana's head and climbed over his body.

On her knees, she bent forward, raising her ass in the air, her pussy in perfect position over his mouth, and she lay her head down on his lower abdomen. His cock was right in front of her face. Kyra would be stroking and sucking him again in no time at all.

RayAnne took her position behind Kyra. The lips of her lover's pussy were flushed pink and moist with her arousal, her clit distended ever so slightly from its hood, the tight pucker of her asshole amazingly perfect.

At the sight of Kyra bared and wide open to her, beyond magnificent and intensely erotic, RayAnne almost growled.

Unable to help herself, she dropped to her knees. Taking Kyra's full ass cheeks in her palms, she squeezed, spreading them apart before licking through her wet slit.

The sweet flavor of cotton-candy coated her tongue. RayAnne moaned and swallowed and then stroked her tongue over Kyra's asshole.

"Oh, yes. Baby, yes!" Kyra whipped her head back, her long hair reaching her lower back.

"Mmm." RayAnne smacked Kyra's ass hard. Urging Kyra forward a little, she focused on Dana. His eyes were closed, and that wouldn't do at all. The venom she'd given him didn't cause a human to pass out. "Dana, open your eyes."

"Oh yeah, *fucccckkkk!*" He arched on the ottoman and raised his arms. He tried to grab Kyra's thighs, but his wrists were still cuffed. "God, your mouth…"

Unsure what was happening, RayAnne peered between his

and Kyra's bodies. A laugh burst out of her. Kyra was sucking his dick again, moving him in and out of her mouth like her immortal life depended on it. That was one sure way to wake a man up.

She bent to his ear. "You like that mouth on your prick, don't you?"

He didn't answer, only shook his head in undeniable agreement.

"Good. Open your eyes and see what awaits you."

"Free my hands. Will you, pleas—oh my God… I need to touch her."

"I don't believe you need to touch her. What you need to do is suck that pretty swollen clit of hers while I fuck her with this thick dildo." RayAnne got to her feet and positioned the head of the dildo at the mouth of Kyra's cunt.

"What're you—" He tilted his head back. "Holy fuck. Really?"

"You're welcome." RayAnne thrust deep, parting Kyra's swollen folds.

Kyra screamed around Dana's cock, and RayAnne landed another slap on her ass. "I believe you can watch me fuck her while you do as I instructed you to." She pulled out and then thrust deep again.

Kyra let out another guttural moan, which morphed into a yell. RayAnne couldn't see for sure, but based on Kyra's reaction, Dana had finally sucked her clit between his lips.

A sudden sensation on her leg caught her attention, and she glanced down, finding Dana had started caressing her inner thigh with the back of one of his hands. His restraints wouldn't allow for more than that little touch.

Lust swirled in RayAnne's belly as she fucked Kyra with earnest thrusts. Dana panted and growled below her. With her mouth stuffed full of dick, Kyra moaned and whimpered with each stroke RayAnne delivered with the dildo.

The mouth of her lover's pink cunt swallowed the flesh-colored phallus. Her ass puckered, almost pleading to be played with.

"Jesus Christ, Kyra, your sweet ass is begging for me." Overcome with a need slicing through her to please her girl, RayAnne licked her thumb and pressed it against Kyra's asshole. She wanted to make her mindless, make her beg.

"Yes, baby. Please, may I have more?"

"That's my girl." She pressed her thumb inside, past the tight outer ring of muscles.

"Holy shit, I'm going to come again!" His words came out in a strangled cry.

"Come all you want, just don't stop sucking that perfect clit." She thrust again, her own cunt spasming at the sight of Kyra's juices glistening on the dildo. "Her sweetness is running right into your mouth, isn't it?"

Dana said nothing. Instead, his muffled yell reached her ears, and he scratched at her inner thigh before finally getting a hold of her leg, gripping her tight.

Kyra threw her head back and screamed, her orgasm rocking her body. RayAnne buried her thumb deeper in Kyra's ass and continued drilling into her lover's cunt with the phallus, her hips slapping against Kyra's full ass cheeks.

RayAnne took hold of Kyra's long hair and yanked her head back farther.

Kyra shook, her orgasm still rolling through her.

RayAnne bent over her and sank her fangs into her neck.

And then RayAnne came—no cock, no mouth, no physical stimulation. Her cunt clenched in on itself, spasming over and over and over again as the room spun around her, and Kyra's sweet blood flowed down her throat.

———

Kyra

DANA'S CUM dripped down Kyra's chin, and her orgasm went on and on, her pussy clenching in rapid spasms around the dildo buried inside her channel.

The pressure in her ass from RayAnne's thumb and RayAnne's needlepoint fangs, still deep in Kyra's throat, heightened the already overwhelming sensations.

Impaled in every way. Exactly how she loved to be.

Dana moaned and then let out a curse as Kyra did her best not to neglect him, to keep stroking his softening shaft. But she could barely focus, her body doing what it needed to do, drowning her in wave after wave of ecstasy.

RayAnne withdrew her fangs from Kyra's throat, licked over the puncture wounds, and then released the hold on Kyra's hair. Free to fall forward, she licked down the length of Dana's shaft and let out a moan when RayAnne withdrew the thick dildo from her cunt.

Without warning, RayAnne licked the mouth of Kyra's pussy.

Kyra shuddered her skin tingling, and then sucked Dana's cock between her lips. His hips shot off the cushion. His cock began to thicken once more.

The man's stamina and rebound time amazed her. He had to be in his mid-forties, give or take, yet he fucked like a horny, wet behind the ears twenty-year-old.

Maybe he'd taken some Viagra, she wondered, thinking he might need it. Not that she cared, though. Between RayAnne and her, he *would* need it.

RayAnne moved to Dana's feet and nodded at Kyra before climbing between his legs. RayAnne spread his thighs.

Kyra slid her mouth to the ridge and suckled the head. At the same time, he licked her clit. She moaned.

RayAnne bent forward and dragged her tongue over his balls. Dana's hot breath blasted over her labia, and she wanted to scream. Instead, she sucked harder.

She and RayAnne were practically nose-to-nose; Kyra slid

her mouth down his length and then back up again. RayAnne suckled his tight sac, taking both globes into her mouth. Dana stopped lapping at her cunt, but his warm breaths caressed her pussy while his hips rose and fell in time with the attention they gave him.

He tasted better than most mortals she'd been with, and she couldn't get enough of him. A deep-seated desire to sink her fangs into his cock, tapping the thick vein running up the shaft, rolled through her. She closed her eyes, trying to tamp down the desire. Most human men didn't take too kindly to that sort of thing.

When she regained some control, she opened her eyes. RayAnne wore a devious smile before she pierced his inner thigh, her fangs disappearing into his flesh.

"Oh, fuck! Yes, goddammit!" Dana's drove his tongue into Kyra's pussy.

The carnal need to taste his blood rose hard and fast, bulldozing over her prior effort to quell it. Kyra slipped him free of her mouth, fisted his prick in her hand and stroked from base to tip.

RayAnne shifted his opposite leg wider, offering to share, and Kyra stretched forward and sank her fangs deep into his bare inner thigh. Dana's hips jerked up, his cock sliding through Kyra's fist before he dropped down again and repeated the motion. His hot blood flowed over Kyra's tongue, down her throat, and her eyes rolled back in her head.

"That's enough, love." RayAnne ran a calming touch over the back of Kyra's hair and then down her back. Kyra shivered at the contact, every inch of her skin in a highly sensitized state.

She nodded, freed her fangs, and sealed the wounds with her tongue. Dana's cock was still hard as she let him go and moved off him.

Her legs wobbled a bit when she stood, and RayAnne steadied her, and then licked up Kyra's chin before taking her in a deep kiss. When they moved apart and turned to face Dana, his eyes were glazed but trained on them.

"Still know your name?" RayAnne climbed onto the ottoman and straddled his hips. "Kyra, release his wrists, please."

He chuckled, a lazy grin parting his lips. "Yes."

Kyra circled the ottoman and did as RayAnne asked. Her baby was about to take his cock inside her sweet pussy, something she rarely did. She must be just as aroused and caught up in the haze that surrounded Kyra.

Dana brought his arms forward and massaged each wrist before flexing and cracking them. Kyra knelt at his head and massaged his shoulders.

In this spot, she'd be able to watch as his prick slid inside RayAnne—a sight she didn't want to miss. The idea amped her up even further. Knowing his hard length would be coated with RayAnne's honeysuckle flavor made her want to climb up there and lick both RayAnne's cunt and his cock as it slid in and out of her.

She held back, though, knowing she couldn't—not without permission anyway.

"Stay where you are, love. But use your fingers to pleasure yourself while you watch." RayAnne licked her lips and positioned the head of his dick at her opening.

"Can I touch you?" Dana hovered his palms above RayAnne's thighs.

"Yes." RayAnne slid down, inch by slow inch.

Kyra focused on her face and then her eyes, and they locked gazes.

He moved his palms up RayAnne's thighs and exhaled a ragged breath. When she'd fully seated herself, he gripped her hips. Kyra's juices dripped down her thigh. Unable to hold off any longer, she found her clit with her fingers and rubbed it in slow, consistent circles.

RayAnne closed her eyes and started riding him. She undulated her hips, cupping her pert breasts in her palms.

"My God, you're tight." Dana ran his hands up RayAnne's torso and then covered her hands with his own. RayAnne pulled hers away, and he gripped her breasts, kneading them and then pinching her nipples.

"One of my finer points." She rolled her pelvis.

Kyra rubbed her clit faster, the erotic scene before her sending fires of lust blazing through her. She scraped a fang over her bottom lip, knowing she'd be able to tap the vein on the other side of his neck soon enough.

Chapter Seven

RayAnne

RAYANNE ROCKED her hips forward and back, enjoying the feel of Dana's cock buried deep and the continuous stimulation her clit received by keeping her pelvis tight to his. Dana shifted his hips in perfect sync with her undulations. She had to admit, even if only to herself, the man knew how to move.

With her hands propped on his chest, she held Kyra's gaze, moaning whenever her lover did, unable to see but knowing Kyra rubbed her clit. The beautifully soft, aroused look on Kyra's face sent RayAnne's thoughts tumbling into the connection between them.

She loved Kyra with a depth she hadn't thought possible when she was human. They'd been together for just over thirty years now, and RayAnne couldn't imagine this existence without her. Best friend, lover and partner. Their arrangement made this life—or existence, rather—bearable.

Dana's hands tightened on her hips, jerking her attention back to him.

She bent forward and pressed her chest to his. With her lips poised above his, she snaked her tongue out and licked over his bottom lip. "What is it, hmm? You want it harder? Rougher?"

"Yes." He flexed his hands on her again.

"Mmm." RayAnne raised her ass in the air. "Show me."

Dana slid his hands around and gripped the back of her thighs and then thrust his hips, slamming his cock inside her while slapping her down against him. Hard, fast and deliberate. RayAnne raised her gaze to Kyra and threaded her fingers into the back of his hair.

"Let me suck your nipples, lover." RayAnne licked her lips, the need to come building inside her like a storm. Kyra inched forward and cupped one large breast in her palm, offering it to RayAnne. She dragged her tongue over one peeked tip before sucking the tight areola between her fangs. Dana continued drilling into her, and her cunt clenched around his shaft.

"Fuck. Your cunt…"

RayAnne flicked Kyra's nipple and then pulled her mouth away. "Spread some of your sweetness on there for me. I need you on my tongue."

Kyra buried two fingers in her cunt and coated the taut pink bud with her juices.

RayAnne licked and sucked every bit of it and then pierced the tender flesh with her fangs. Kyra's flavor exploded through her.

Dana took one of RayAnne's breasts in hand and squeezed, lapping at her nipple. With his other, he pressed two fingers, slippery with her juices, into her asshole.

RayAnne's orgasm barreled forward and detonated like a bomb. She screamed around Kyra's breast, and Dana fucked her harder, his own climax exploding out of him. Spinning and spinning, wave after wave, she came. Her cunt contracted around his prick with each impalement.

Drowning in the sensations, RayAnne closed her eyes and tried to ground herself. The distant sounds of Kyra, her little whimpers between the endearments she whispered to RayAnne, became the only thing she could hear.

Dana stopped moving, and RayAnne removed her fangs from her lover's breast. When most of her senses returned, she looked down at him. He'd passed out. *Shit.*

"Did you kill him?"

"Not yet. Unless he had a heart attack." RayAnne smirked.

"That's silly. I can hear his heart beating." Kyra giggled. "Maybe we should get him some juice or something."

"Of course." She pressed a kiss to Kyra's lips. "Go grab that, and I'll rouse him."

"I think you roused him too much. Be right back." Kyra tossed her a devious look and walked out of the room.

RayAnne rose off Dana's still body. Kyra was right. He hadn't had a heart attack, but he'd definitely passed out. Not surprising, considering she'd just wrung a third orgasm from him.

"Dana?" She tapped his cheek. "Wake up." He didn't respond, so she slapped him. Not too hard, but enough to make her chuckle.

He regained consciousness with a gasp for air and then rubbed his cheek. "Did you just hit me?"

"Don't be a baby. You passed out, and that's not acceptable. Kyra's getting you some juice. I'm not nearly done with you, so we need to keep your blood sugar up."

He rubbed his palms over his face and yawned. "Just let me rest a few minutes."

"As you wish, but drink the juice first."

Kyra returned and handed her a small glass of orange juice. RayAnne took a seat next to him. "Sit up and drink this."

He groaned but did as she asked. When he finished, he handed the glass back to RayAnne and then lay down again.

"What's he doing?" Kyra pursed her lips into a pout.

"Don't worry, lover. He's just going to rest for a few minutes." Getting to her feet, she set the glass down on a small table and moved back to Kyra. "While he does, let's you and me play in the meantime." She ran her hands up Kyra's torso and kissed her.

"That sounds nice." Kyra smiled, and then RayAnne kissed her again, their tongues tangling.

RayAnne moaned and cupped Kyra's soft, deliciously wet folds in her palm. She had to taste her, had to drive her mindless before letting her come.

Breaking the kiss, RayAnne glanced over at the toys laid out on the sideboard. Ah, yes, the blindfold and vibrators would be perfect. After retrieving the items, she returned to Kyra. "Lie down on the ground. Arms to your sides, palms up, legs spread."

Kyra nodded and assumed the position.

Kneeling beside, she fastened the blindfold and then pressed another kiss to her lover's perfect lips. "So beautiful, my love."

Kyra smiled. "Thank you."

RayAnne moved between Kyra's parted legs and took her large breasts in her palms. So perfect. So full and completely natural. She massaged them, squeezing and pressing them together. Leaning forward, she licked over each perfect taut nipple. Giving equal attention to both, teasing them with the tip of a fang.

Kyra shivered, whimpering with each scrape of RayAnne's fang.

"Heaven to watch your nipples get even harder as if they were reaching to be closer to my mouth." RayAnne sucked one tight bud, pinched and rolled the other between her fingertips.

When her breathing became more moans than anything else, RayAnne pulled away and stared down at Kyra's breasts. She ran her palms around the outside and then back to the insides of them, rubbing and gripping the full globes. Satisfaction zinged through her at the bright pink shade that rose on Kyra's pale skin. Her lover had taken enough blood from Dana to allow her skin to respond the way a mortal's would.

RayAnne reached for one of the vibrators, turned it on and circled a nipple with it.

Kyra arched her body, whimpering from the contact.

She continued down the center of Kyra's stomach, following the path she drew with her palm, exploring the tight stomach muscles before settling the end of the vibrator against Kyra's swollen clit.

Kyra raised her knees and tilted her pelvis forward.

"Stay still."

"Yes, baby." Kyra went still, and RayAnne knew she was once again ready to surrender her body and mind.

Kyra was RayAnne's. Hers to control. Hers to fuck. Hers to take care of.

Hers.

And she owned every inch of Kyra's beautiful body.

Kyra

KYRA'S BODY buzzed with arousal. All her senses heightened to the point of madness due to the blindfold.

RayAnne held the tip of the vibrator to Kyra's clit. The constant vibration sent waves of arousal pounding through her, hurtling Kyra toward the edge of another orgasm. But she knew RayAnne wouldn't allow her to come yet.

Kyra bit down on her bottom lip, panting and moaning, doing everything in her power not to move her body.

"Would you like to come, lover?"

"Yes." She nodded. "Please, may I?"

RayAnne chuckled. "Not yet."

Kyra sucked in a deep breath. Agitation or frustration pulsed through her. It was hard, but the truth was, Kyra loved it. Pride and satisfaction doused her agitation. She loved giving over control to RayAnne. She loved when RayAnne dictated her pleasure.

And she loved RayAnne.

She loved RayAnne's grim moods, her morose attitude, and the lack of conscience RayAnne insisted she had no possession of. Which was valid proof her baby did, in fact, have a conscience—Kyra couldn't stop the smile that spread across her lips at the thought.

"What's got you smiling?"

"Nothing."

RayAnne pulled the vibrator away and then slapped Kyra's pussy. With a scream, her hips shot off the floor. Sweet hell, the sting and then the radiating heat had her clit pulsing for more.

"Still your body. Now, tell me."

Kyra swallowed. "I love you, baby. That's all."

"Mmm." RayAnne pressed a soft kiss to her lips.

Kyra closed her eyes behind the blindfold, accepting the gentle yet erotic affection.

RayAnne pressed her thigh against Kyra's core. "Rub against me. I want to feel your sweet honey all over my thigh."

Kyra accepted her kiss once again and rocked her hips, rubbing her pussy against RayAnne's toned thigh. She wanted to touch her, wanted to slide a hand between them and return the attention to RayAnne. Instead, she waited, knowing if she did, everything would be more incredible than it already was.

RayAnne lapped at her lips, nipped them, drawing little trickles of blood that passed between them while Kyra rolled her pelvis, getting wetter, hotter, almost losing control. Her orgasm rode to the surface faster than lightning, and Kyra broke the kiss and cried out.

"You want to come so bad, don't you?" RayAnne crooned. Her lips grazed the shell of Kyra's ear.

"Yes, baby. So bad."

"Not yet. But soon."

Kyra whimpered and gasped for breath. She felt RayAnne move, and then the vibrator was slid deep inside her channel. "Oh God!"

RayAnne sucked Kyra's clit between her lips.

"I can't. RayAnne, I can't—" She thrashed her head side to side.

"Come for me, lover." RayAnne slid the vibrator in and out and sucked her clit.

Thank fuck! Shockwaves rocketed through Kyra's cunt and as her orgasm exploded, she clenched down around the vibrator. Kyra couldn't stop the scream that punched out of her or the waves of what felt like an endless climax from rolling through her.

The distant sound of something registered in her ears a few moments later.

Someone was clapping.

"That was fucking incredible."

"You're welcome." RayAnne gave one last lick through Kyra's folds and then tugged the blindfold down Kyra's face.

Kyra blinked and looked over to find Dana sitting on the ottoman, clapping his hands, dick fully hard.

Hmm. It was time for the man to forget his name, and by the look on RayAnne's face, she intended to be the one to take him to that place.

Chapter Eight

RayAnne

RAYANNE FASTENED the strap-on harness around her hips once more. It was time for Dana to have a taste of heaven—or hell, depending on how receptive he was.

An odd agitation had risen in her when she realized he'd been watching them. Not that she cared when people watched her fuck her woman, but the deal was RayAnne had to be the one who invited it or granted permission.

Neither had happened. Therefore, Mr. Businessman needed to be taught a lesson.

"On your knees on top of the ottoman, Kyra." She walked toward them both. "Dana, get to your feet."

Dana stared at her, a look of uncertainty in his eyes.

Kyra climbed onto the ottoman next to him and ran her palm up his thigh to his dick. The show of affection was enough to distract him from whatever assessment he was making. He leaned to the side and pressed his lips to Kyra's, and she deepened the kiss, threading her fingers through his silver-tinted hair.

When she pulled away, he was breathless and looked a whole bunch more compliant.

RayAnne held her hand out to him. He took it and rose to his feet. She led him around the edge of the ottoman as Kyra got into position.

"Chin up, Kyra." RayAnne pressed her chest against Dana's back and urged him forward. Taking his erect penis in her hand, she stroked him from base to tip. Dana exhaled a hard breath, and a bead of pre-cum emerged from the tip. "That's it. Mmm." She brushed her lips over his neck. "I see the juice helped you."

"I didn't really need it." He shifted his hips forward.

Such a good little helper he was. And an arrogant one, too.

RayAnne shifted him farther forward. "Open up, Kyra."

Kyra smiled and licked her lips, and then opened her mouth like a good girl. RayAnne fed his hard cock to her soft, welcoming lips. Lucky bastard had no idea the gifts he'd been given tonight. But he would soon enough.

"You want to fuck her, don't you?"

Dana moaned an unintelligible yes, panting with each pass of Kyra's brilliant mouth.

"Greedy." She dragged her tongue over his neck. The pulse beat hard against her tongue, and RayAnne's fangs ached for another taste. "You've already fucked her mouth twice. Or has it been three times? Hmm…but now you want to fuck her sweet cotton-candy-flavored cunt don't you?"

"Oh, God, yes!"

RayAnne scraped a fang over his throat. "Do you want it bad enough to beg for it?"

"Yes. Yes! Please let me fuck her pussy."

RayAnne smiled and nipped at his neck. "You impress me, Dana. I would've thought you a man above begging."

"I'm a—" He gasped. "I'm a smart man. I do what I need

to in order to close the deal. Whatever—fuck—whatever it takes."

"Very well. Take him close, Kyra. If he starts to come, hold him." RayAnne caught Kyra's gaze, and she blinked her eyes, acknowledging the command. She returned to Dana's neck, licking and sucking over the tender area. She was going to bite him again; needed to give him a little more of her venom in order to get him lost within the ecstasy flooding all of them.

Dana moaned, panted, groaned, and gritted his teeth while Kyra sucked his dick like it was her last meal. He was getting close, the tendons in his neck strung tight, perspiration beading on his forehead and chest.

RayAnne reached around the front of him and cupped his balls in her palm. She massaged, tugged and then tilted his head to the side and sank her fangs in.

The same sweet sangria flavor flowed down her throat. So strange. He didn't appear to be of ethnic origin. But then again, sometimes it was hard to tell with a person. She glanced down at Kyra. Her lover had pulled him from her mouth and was squeezing the head of his cock in her palm.

"Hold it, Dana! Don't come." Kyra said. "I want you to fuck me and then come for me. So, do not. You can do it; breathe. Breathe."

Fuck sake, RayAnne loved her woman. Always in sync with each other. So opposite, yet in complete coordination. RayAnne closed her eyes, savoring the warmth in her heart and the taste of Dana's blood.

Savoring everything about this moment.

Kyra

KYRA KEPT her gaze locked with Dana's.

Sia's *Cellophane* played through the room, mingling with the sounds coming from Dana's mouth. Various looks of rapture passed over his features, from pain to lust and, finally, ease. He'd managed to hold back his orgasm, which was surprising.

Most mortal men had a hard time doing that, especially if it was something they didn't do often. But for all she knew, maybe he did. Pretty much everything about this guy had been unexpected.

She'd joked with RayAnne about him being a freak, but maybe he did have a little inner freak going on that he might not even be aware of.

Dana's breathing evened out. RayAnne was still at his vein, and now a calm, blissful look took up residence in his eyes. Kyra bent her head, closed her eyes and took him into her mouth again. The sharp intake of breath coming from him stirred the large pool of lust in her stomach. Soon, she'd have him inside her cunt. Very soon.

"Release him, Kyra. It's time."

Kyra glanced up and slid him free of her mouth.

RayAnne licked over the punctures on his neck and then led him around the ottoman. "Roll to your back, my love."

Kyra nodded and wiped her chin. Her cunt ached to be filled by him, her clit pulsing at a steady beat. After she rolled over, she watched RayAnne kiss him, her jaw working as their tongues clashed together.

Kyra had to stifle a moan at the sight. Devil's angels, she was ready.

"Now you can fuck her. While I have my fun with you."

Dana smiled. "What kind of fun?"

"Don't worry, I'm sure you're going to love it. You've loved everything we've done with you and for you so far, right? Don't start questioning now. You'll ruin all the fun. And you did say you wanted to forget your name. Now's your chance,

Mr. Executive." RayAnne stroked his saliva slicked cock once, then twice before kissing him again.

Dana moved onto the ottoman between Kyra's parted thighs. RayAnne grabbed one of the large wedge pillows from the corner and placed it under Kyra's bottom. In this position, her hips would be elevated off the cushion, which would force Dana's ass in the air so RayAnne could have her way with him.

Dana stayed on his knees, staring down at her exposed pussy.

"She's pretty there, isn't she?" RayAnne stroked her fingers over Kyra's mound.

"Very." He smiled.

"Prettiest cunt I've ever laid my eyes on." RayAnne raised her hand and then delivered a slap to Kyra's pussy.

Kyra cried out but kept her body still. The sting radiated through her, and her clit pulsed harder.

RayAnne chuckled. "You want more, don't you, my love?"

"Yes. Please, yes." Kyra licked her bottom lip.

RayAnne delivered another slap.

This time, Kyra was unable to stop her hips from rising off the pillow. The heady pleasure/pain was just too much, too overwhelming. She gritted her teeth and moaned, knowing her juices now dripped down her ass. God, she needed to be fucked.

Dana's eyes were wide as silver dollars. "My God, look at that." He ran his fingers through her folds, teasing the mouth of her cunt, and then dragged them down to her asshole. "Most amazing thing I've ever seen."

"I agree." RayAnne moved behind him, a bottle of lube in her hand. "Dana, have you ever had your ass played with? Ever had that nice little male G-spot, also known as the prostate gland, stimulated?"

"Um…" He dragged his eyes away from Kyra's pussy and looked over his shoulder at RayAnne. "I—"

"It's a perfectly natural thing, you know." RayAnne tsk'd. "Don't neglect my girl. I do believe she's ready for you."

Dana nodded and turned back to Kyra.

"Come on, let me feel you inside me. I need you." Kyra palmed her breasts and squeezed them together.

It wasn't a lie; she did need him. She needed his throbbing dick as much as she needed his vein. And she was done waiting for both.

RayAnne

RAYANNE PRESSED herself against Dana's back and smoothed her hands down his chest as he inched forward.

With his cock fisted in his palm, he rubbed the head over Kyra's swollen clit. Apparently, he was going to take his time, tease her a little before finally sinking inside. He might be an arrogant executive, but at least he knew how to treat a woman sexually.

Kyra let out a little sigh when he penetrated her with just the head, and RayAnne ran her hands down his abdomen to his balls. He moved in and out of Kyra's pussy in short thrusts, and RayAnne massaged his sac.

"Fuck, that feels so damn good."

"Mmm. Know what else feels good?"

"I have a feeling you're going to show me."

She pulled away and squeezed a healthy amount of lube onto two of her fingers. "Fuck her as good as you fucked me, and I *will* show you."

"That's a given." Dana slid his arms under Kyra's legs and thrust into her.

"Oh, God, yes!" Kyra moaned.

"Yeah, baby. Your pussy is like velvet. Rub your sweet little clit for me."

RayAnne moved against his back again and then slid her fingers between his ass cheeks. "Just relax and enjoy," she whispered against his ear. He tensed at first but then relaxed, and she massaged his tight, puckered hole. "That's it."

"Holy shit." Dana rocked his hips forward, and RayAnne slid two fingers inside his asshole. "I've never— Oh fuck, yes!"

Kyra let out a whimper. "Fuck me harder, Dana!"

Dana bent over Kyra, just as RayAnne knew he would, putting himself in the perfect position for her to fuck him, too.

Kyra wrapped her legs around his lower back and gripped his ass with her hands. RayAnne smiled as Kyra dug her nails in and spread his ass cheeks apart.

Perfect. God, her girl was fucking perfect and knew exactly what RayAnne needed her to do.

She knelt on the ottoman behind him and added another finger to his ass. Dana cried out, fucking Kyra's cunt, but didn't stop. RayAnne thrust her fingers in and out of his ass, spreading them apart, readying his tight hole for the dildo.

Kyra let out her first scream, coming around his dick.

"Yeah. Fuck, yeah. That's it." Dana slowed his thrusts and ground his pelvis against Kyra.

"You feel her milking your dick?" She squirted more lube into her palm and spread it over the dildo. "Almost enough to make you forget your name, huh?"

"Never felt anything like the two of you." He thrust in and out again, his hips slapping against Kyra.

"I know. And you never will again." RayAnne pressed the head of the dildo against his asshole.

"Wait, are you going—"

RayAnne peeked around the side of him. Kyra had locked Dana in a kiss, her tongue buried in his mouth. He hadn't stopped fucking her, though his thrusting slowed, which, again, worked perfect. On his retreat, RayAnne slid the tip in and then continued deeper when he pressed into Kyra again.

"*Oh, my fucking*—" He froze.

"Just breathe." RayAnne smoothed her hand down his back. "Just breathe and let yourself feel."

He let out a gasp and took a few deep breaths, groaning with each one, and then finally resumed fucking Kyra.

RayAnne held still, letting him set the pace and impale himself with each thrust into her lover.

Kyra's moans grew louder, as did his. RayAnne's clit throbbed with each whimper and grunt from the two of them. Pleasure and satisfaction raced through her, and they found a rhythm, three bodies slapping against each other, two in a mad frenzy speeding toward a cataclysmic orgasm.

Kyra came again. Her muffled scream told RayAnne she'd bit into Dana's neck, sucking at his vein while he fucked into her, his own scream echoing around them as his climax hit.

"That's it, come for me." RayAnne gripped his ass cheeks and spread them apart, watching as she sank deep into his ass with the strap-on.

Dana jerked, his body going rigid. Kyra's legs were still wrapped tight around him, but now she had one hand sunk deep in his hair, her fingers gripping the strands tight, keeping his head turned to one side as she drank from him. Dana thrust once more and then went boneless, collapsing onto Kyra.

Pleased with herself, RayAnne slid the dildo out of his ass and then stepped away to remove the harness and grab a towel for him. When she returned, both he and Kyra were in the same position. Dana's eyes were closed, and he wasn't moving.

What the hell?

RayAnne bent over them and looked down at Kyra. *Oh, no!* "Kyra! Oh, shit! Kyra!"

Kyra opened her eyes and gazed up at RayAnne, pupils fully dilated. She looked completely blood-drunk and almost feral.

"Kyra, love, let him go."

Kyra let out a small growl, her fangs still buried deep, and gripped Dana tighter to her body.

Fucking hell, if she didn't get her to release him quickly, she was going to kill him. The last thing they needed was a dead businessman on their hands. Especially one as well-known as Dana Richards was.

Fear vibrated through RayAnne's limbs, and she knelt down beside them. "Kyra, listen to me." Kyra shook her head and took a deep draw. "Kyra Lee James, you let him go this instant, or you're going to kill him. Is that what you want?" She placed her hand on the side of Kyra's face. "Let him go, lover."

Kyra closed her eyes for what felt like an eternity before finally pulling her mouth from his neck. The puncture wounds she'd made oozed blood, and RayAnne jerked Dana away from Kyra's grasp, rolled him onto his back and then sealed them with her tongue.

Dana looked gray, his lips blue.

Fucking hell, son-of-a-bitch, motherfucker, son of a whore! This was not happening!

"Wake up, Dana!" RayAnne slapped him across the face. Which was stupid because he wasn't passed out, he was dying. CPR wouldn't help with blood loss. Besides, neither of them knew CPR...which was also stupid because you'd think after being on the planet for so damn long, it'd be a skill a person—or vampire—might acquire. *Fuck, focus RayAnne!* "Dana! Wake the fuck up!" She slapped him again.

Kyra had moved off the ottoman and was now curled around herself on the floor, rocking back and forth, crying and babbling something along the lines of, "I didn't mean to. He tasted so good. It was an accident."

"Get it together, Kyra! I can't have you losing your shit right now." RayAnne glared at her, anger replacing the fear.

"Don't yell at me." Kyra wiped her wet cheeks.

"He's dying. Forgive me if I'm a little short-tempered with you."

Dammit, she never should've let Kyra bring him home. It was too risky. Shit like this didn't happen all that often, but when it did, it was usually with a more anonymous or disposable person.

Dana Richards was neither anonymous nor disposable.

Chapter Nine

Kyra

Kyra sat on the floor a few feet away from Dana's still body on the ottoman. She hadn't meant to take so much from him. She just…she lost herself in the maelstrom of lust and sexual intensity of the moment.

RayAnne had been fucking his ass; he was fucking Kyra's cunt; and everything just went nuts from there. And she honestly had no idea what'd happened until she heard RayAnne calling her name. She'd lost all control of herself, and the amount of focus it took to regain her composure scared the shit out of her. What was it with his blood? Or his tongue? Or his dick? None of it made sense…

"We're going to have to turn him."

RayAnne's voice tore her from her thoughts. "What?"

"Get up. We're going to have to turn him."

"But… we can't."

"Yeah? You got a better idea? Call me selfish, but I'd rather not have to move. I kinda love where we live."

"You hate our job, though."

"Beside the point! Will you please get up and fucking help me?" RayAnne glared at her.

"All right. I'm sorry, RayAnne. Stop yelling." Kyra got to her feet, her legs shaking, and moved to the ottoman.

"We're doing this together. At this point, his pulse is so weak, I don't even know if he'll survive the transition."

"Together, like you mean, we're both going to give him blood?"

"You got it." RayAnne bit into her own wrist.

"Has that ever been done before? Two people turning a human at the same time?"

RayAnne shrugged, pried Dana's mouth open and pressed her wrist to his lips. "Not that I've heard. I'll tell you when it's your turn, okay?"

Kyra stared down at Dana's ashen face. Was he even swallowing? Sadness pooled in her stomach, making her want to vomit up the blood she'd just stolen from him. Crap, she felt really bad. She kinda liked him, had hoped they'd be able to do this again. But then again, if he survived being turned, maybe they would. Hmmm…

"Kyra, okay?" RayAnne's words were loud and harsh.

She looked up at RayAnne. "Okay." She started to cry.

"Lover, stop crying; it's going to be all right." RayAnne bent over Dana's still form and kissed her soft on the lips.

"I love you."

"I love you, too. Now, go ahead and bite your wrist and place it on his mouth."

Kyra did as RayAnne said and held her bleeding wrist to Dana's lips. RayAnne massaged his throat, the way a person did to a pet when they were trying to get them to swallow a pill or medicine. This was crazy, and all Kyra could do was pray it worked. Fear raced through her, erasing all traces of the pleasure she experienced not ten minutes before. She guessed they'd know if he lived or died in the next twelve hours anyway.

"I hope this works."

RayAnne looked at her. "If not, we'll be digging a hole somewhere in the mountains."

———

RayAnne

RayAnne got the bed ready and then turned the lock around on the door. Couldn't have him getting up in the middle of the day when they were both still sleeping and wandering off…of course, if he transitioned, he'd not make it very far.

RayAnne shuddered at the thought and walked back into the library. Kyra was poised on the edge of the ottoman, brushing the hair off Dana's forehead, a look of concern blanking her features. She knew Kyra felt bad about what she'd done. And she'd spend the next ten years beating herself up if this little plan didn't work, maybe even if it did.

"He's just so still."

"I know. But that part's normal." RayAnne smoothed her palm down the back of Kyra's hair. "Ready to help me carry him into bed?"

"We're keeping him with us upstairs, right?"

"No." She moved to his head. "Grab his legs."

"Why not?" Kyra moved to his feet.

"Because there's nothing more we can do. We'll lock him in the guest room, and at sunset, we'll come downstairs and check him." She gripped him under his arms, and they both lifted.

"And then what?"

"Then, he'll either be a vampire or he'll be dead." RayAnne walked backward out of the room.

After they laid him down on the bed, she watched from the doorway while Kyra tucked the covers around him. She bent and kissed his forehead and then made her way to RayAnne.

"I'm scared." Kyra frowned.

"Me too." RayAnne cupped Kyra's cheek. "Go on upstairs and shower. I'll be there in a minute." Kyra nodded and stepped away.

RayAnne glanced at Dana's still form once more and then closed the door and locked it.

Chapter Ten

RayAnne

RAYANNE ROLLED over in bed and stretched an arm out, seeking Kyra, but found only sheets. "Kyra?"

The sun had just barely set, and concern sent ice water slicing through her veins. She sat up and glanced around the room, peering through the darkness at the open primary bathroom door. Her love, who usually slept later than RayAnne due to her younger vampire age, was nowhere to be found.

RayAnne rose from the bed, donned her silk robe and moved to the bedroom door. They had enough shades and drapes throughout the lower level, plus a dark tint on the windows to keep her safe from any sun rays, so she wasn't concerned. But during the full-on daylight, they still had to be careful. With no idea when Kyra had gotten up and left their bed, she was, however, more than a little worried about her. What if Dana had transitioned but was mad from being so far gone before they started?

She padded down the curved staircase and through the foyer to the hallway leading to the guest bedroom. Pausing at the door, she listened. A faint moan filtered through the thick wood panel. "You have got to be kidding me." RayAnne turned the handle and opened the door.

The sight she was greeted with made her both roll her eyes in annoyance and breathe—not that she actually needed to breathe—a sigh of relief.

Kyra was riding Dana, body straddling his hips, head thrown back in the throes of ecstasy. And he was sitting upright, one arm wrapped tight around her lover's lower back. With his free hand, Dana had a death grip around one full breast as he sucked her nipple, blood dripping from the corners of his mouth.

"Sweet hell, really?" RayAnne crossed her arms.

Kyra's head snapped up, and she looked over at RayAnne, but her hips didn't miss a beat, continuing to rock back and forth, fucking him. "He survived! And he's hungry."

"I can see that."

Kyra smiled and cupped the back of his head. "That's it, sweetheart, keep feeding." She kissed the top of his head.

He spared RayAnne a glance before withdrawing his fangs from Kyra's breast and then sought her mouth for a kiss. Jesus, new vampires could be insatiable—for both sex and blood. The two went hand in hand for the first few days.

He'd survived for sure and appeared to be adjusting quite well. *Amazing.* RayAnne couldn't help but wonder what he'd taste like now. Or what he'd fuck like, though she was getting a pretty good idea. He more than held his own as a human. As a vampire, he'd be a force to be reckoned with—a *fucking* force to be reckoned with might be a better description.

Kyra broke from the kiss and cupped one of her breasts, offering it to him. Dana snarled and then latched on like a damn babe, one with very sharp fangs. Kyra held a hand out to RayAnne. "Come here, baby. Join us."

RayAnne dropped her arms to her sides, unable to refuse such a sweet request, and untied her robe, letting it fall to the floor at her feet. She moved onto the bed beside them and then ran her palm down Dana's arm. His skin was cool and smooth, his muscles more defined since transitioning.

He pulled from Kyra's breast, and laid down flat, and then dragged RayAnne to straddle his face. *All righty then.* The first contact of his tongue along the mouth of her cunt had an uncontrollable moan punching out of her. Then he moved lower, latched onto her clit and sank his fangs into her folds. RayAnne grabbed hold of Kyra's arms, her pussy flooding with her juices, and ground against his mouth while Kyra impaled herself over and over again on his cock.

"Can we keep him?" Kyra gasped a moan.

The room tilted, and RayAnne closed her eyes. She couldn't think about that right now; in fact, she couldn't think of anything except the pleasure flooding her system.

Everything beyond intense, so utterly addicting, she wasn't sure *not* keeping him was even an option she could consider.

Kyra

KYRA LAY DRAPED across Dana's chest in a half-exhausted state. She couldn't remember the last time she felt so drained, but it'd all been worth it.

She'd lost track of how many times she orgasmed as they traded positions, and Dana took turns fucking each of them. One of them getting eaten out, while the other took a cock in a mouth, cunt, or ass, and vice versa. Blood streaked the white sheets of the guest bed, as well as their bodies.

Dana's cum and blood tasted like tropical fruit, and she'd dined on it like the delicacy it was. Kyra was serious when she asked RayAnne if they could keep him.

She really wanted to.

Fucking him was something she could get used to daily. And sucking his prick? Definitely, multiple times a day.

RayAnne moaned, jerking Kyra from her thoughts, and sat up from her curled position beside Dana. She glanced across his body and locked eyes with Kyra.

"So, can we?"

"Can we what?" RayAnne ran her fingers through her long black hair.

Kyra sat up. "Can we keep him?"

"He'll need to stay here for at least a week until he adjusts. But he's not a stray cat, lover. We can't just *keep* him."

"I know he's not a stray cat, but he's just as cute." Kyra shrugged and ran her palm down Dana's chest. "I like him."

RayAnne stood and put on her robe. "It's not really up to us."

"But we're his makers. Isn't he supposed to stay with us?" Kyra lay back down and rested her cheek on his chest.

"That's beside the point."

Dana cleared his throat, and Kyra jerked her head up to look at him. "Anyone care to enlighten me with what you're bickering about?"

"We're not bickering. We don't bicker." RayAnne jutted her chin out and crossed her arms in a defensive stance.

"All women bicker." He was pulling RayAnne's proverbial pigtails, and she was falling for it. Kyra knew it and giggled. "Allow me to settle it for you." He squeezed Kyra's ass, and she giggled again.

"What's that supposed to mean?"

Kyra sat up, wanting to watch the exchange between Dana and RayAnne—which had quickly become entertainment. She could so get used to this.

"Means if I must, I'll stay here. The sex alone is worth the sacrifice."

"Hope you don't mind working nights." RayAnne snorted.

"Good thing I have plenty of business overseas to deal with, right?" He smiled wide, flashing his perfect and very sharp incisors.

RayAnne rested one knee on the bed and leaned over him. She kissed him deep and long, her tongue flicking out over one of his fangs and then nicking his tongue with one her hers.

Dana groaned and tried to pull her fully onto the bed, but RayAnne refused to budge. Instead, she pulled from the kiss and gazed down at him, a demure smile arching her lips. "You're welcome."

"Think you can keep stealing my line, hmm? We'll see." Dana let out a loud laugh, and Kyra couldn't help but laugh with him. Finally, RayAnne, unable to keep her composure, joined in.

Genuine excitement raced through Kyra. Her favorite businessman, Dana Richards, was the perfect addition to their story.

And just like that, the two became three.

About the Author

Dorothy F. Shaw lives in Arizona, where the weather is hot, and the sunsets are always beautiful. She's a self-proclaimed sex scene snob and is proud of it. When she's not writing, she's thinking about writing.

With her ever-open heart, bright red hair, and many colorful tattoos, she truly lives and loves in Technicolor!

Also by Dorothy F. Shaw

Head to my site to find all links to my available backlist:

www.DorothyFShaw.com

This book is a work of fiction. The names, characters, places, and
incidents are products of the writer's imagination or have been used
fictitiously and are not to be construed as real. Any resemblance to
persons, living or dead, actual events, locale or organizations is
entirely coincidental.

Dorothy F. Shaw
Phoenix, Arizona
PLAYTIME
Copyright © 2017 by Dorothy F. Shaw
ISBN-13: 978-0-9978310-7-8
ISBN-10: 0-9978310-7-3
Draft2Digital ISBN-13: 978-0-4630010-7-3
Cover by: Terry "Wookie" Hoffman & Khloe Wren

Red Queen Publications electronic publication: October 2017

Publishing History
Digital 1.0 edition / November 2014
Digital 2.0 edition / October 2017

Red Queen
Publications